NOWHERE TO HIDE

KIM SIGAFUS

7th GENERATION

Summertown, Tennessee

Library of Congress Cataloging-in-Publication Data available upon request.

© 2019 Gary Robinson

Cover and interior design: John Wincek

7th Generation
Book Publishing Company
PO Box 99, Summertown, TN 38483
888-260-8458
bookpubco.com
nativevoicesbooks.com

ISBN: 978-1-939053-21-3

24 23 22 21 20 19   1 2 3 4 5 6 7 8 9

Having been a victim of bullying when I was in school, I dedicate this book to anyone who is dealing with it now. If others tease you for the way you look, talk, act, think, or feel, remember that it's okay to be different. Being different makes you unique.

To anyone who is doing the bullying, think about something Maya Angelou—an American author, actress, screenwriter, dancer, poet, and civil rights activist—once said:

I've learned that people will forget what you said, people will forget what you did, but people will never forget how you made them feel.

It is my hope that everyone who reads this book will stand up and be a light for others.

CONTENTS

NOWHERE TO HIDE

Dealing with Life

Hey, I've been looking for you."

Autumn turned away from her blue school locker to see Sydney Coffman standing there.

"What do you want?" Autumn asked, shutting her locker and giving it a little push. It wouldn't close right, so she opened it back up and shoved it a little harder trying to get it shut. She waited until she heard it click and then twisted the lock before she walked away. Sydney laughed and followed her.

"Only a dummy would have trouble with their locker," Sydney said, falling in step beside her.

Autumn didn't reply as she shifted her heavy backpack to the other shoulder.

"I hear you might be trying out for the play," said Sydney, walking backward in front of her.

"So?"

"With the way you talk, you've got to be kidding. You can't even pronounce the name of the play. It comes out sounding stupid, like 'The Jingle Dreth.'"

Autumn tried to ignore her by walking around her and taking a side hall to the parking lot. Sydney caught up to her and gave her a push.

"Hey, I'm talking to you."

"My mom is waiting in the car."

Sydney laughed, pushing her again. "I don't care."

"Stop it," said Autumn, falling back against the wall. She straightened up and caught a glimpse of a couple of kids coming down the hall toward her. She swung her backpack around and held it in her arms for protection.

Two girls rushed toward Sydney with a grin.

"I see you found Autumn," Bree said. "We were looking for her too."

"Yeah, she's thinking of trying out for the play," replied Sydney. "But I think she might change her mind."

They stared at Autumn's stony face as her gaze fell to the floor. She hugged her backpack tighter to her chest.

"You know that we try out for the fall play every year," said Jayden. "What makes you think you have a chance to get a part?"

"We always get the best parts anyway, so you might as well forget it," added Sydney, and her friends nodded.

"Fine . . . whatever," replied Autumn, heading for the door again. The three girls laughed and walked behind her.

"She's so stupid," Sydney whispered loudly to her friends. "I mean, not only does she talk weird, but she's too stupid to get her homework done. I heard Mr. B. talking to her after class yesterday. She hasn't turned any homework in all week."

"It's none of your business," Autumn shot back, struggling as always with the s sounds in the word. She pushed the door open and stepped outside.

As she ran down the steps and headed for her mother's car, she could hear Sydney yell after her, but she didn't stop.

Autumn headed across the parking lot to a white SUV. Her mother was waiting there with two-year-old Sam, who was crying. Autumn's mother was trying to comfort him.

Autumn opened the front door to see her mother glaring at her.

"Why didn't you answer those nice girls back?" asked her mother, trying to find the pacifier. "If you ignore everybody, you'll never make any friends."

Autumn pushed her shoulder-length black hair out of her eyes and sighed. Her mother had no idea what was going on, and she didn't want to tell her. It would just make matters worse. Better to just keep it to herself, she thought.

She was late getting out of school, and she could tell her mother was mad. Autumn's dark eyes clouded over as she steeled herself for the yelling she knew was coming.

"And where have you been, Autumn Dawn?" her mother asked impatiently. "I've been here for ten minutes." She fumbled with Sam and then spat out, "What is wrong with this kid? He won't quiet down!"

"I had trouble with my locker," Autumn replied as she threw her backpack in the back seat and got into the front seat. "What's wrong with him?" she asked, pointing to her brother.

"He hates that car seat," said her mother. "It's almost too small for him now." She growled and turned around to face forward. "He'll just have to get used to it."

"Maybe he needs a bigger seat," replied Autumn as she leaned over to dig into the diaper bag sitting next to Sam. She handed him his pacifier, then she buckled her seat belt and added, "Maybe we should get one."

Autumn's mother laughed loudly as she shook her head. Her short blonde curls bounced around her heart-shaped face. "No money for that." She started the car and pulled away from the school. "How was your day?" she mumbled.

Autumn glanced over at her. "Same as always. Mom, can we do something fun this weekend?"

"I have to work."

"Oh." Autumn sighed and stared out the window as they drove through town.

Autumn loved living on the White Earth Reservation. Located in the northwest corner of Minnesota, it was beautiful there. There were woods and lakes all around, and Autumn spent most of her time outside.

Her father, Tom, also grew up there. His Ojibwa name meant "One Who Gathers," but everyone called him Tom. The thought of her father made her smile. She'd been told many times that with her black hair and dark brown eyes, she looked just like him.

Autumn sat back in her seat, staring out the window as she thought about him. He liked to tell the story of how he met her mother. His parents were hoping he'd find an Ojibwa girl to marry, but he fell head over heels in love with a girl from Topeka, Kansas, by the name of Melissa Stewart. She had come to the reservation to visit a friend for the summer. Her curly blonde hair set her apart immediately from the dark Native American women he was used to seeing around town. Everyone noticed her, as a matter of fact, and Tom had to work hard to make sure she noticed him in the sea of men trying to get a date with her. Autumn's father told her he won her mother's heart with his charm. Her mother said it was his work ethic and kind heart.

Once they were married, they both worked hard to support their little family. Her mother got a job working at the library, and her father worked for a construction company. They did a lot of things as a family, until her parents' occasional fights turned into an everyday occurrence. When she was younger, he took her fishing. Now she hardly saw him at all.

Autumn sighed and her eyes clouded over as she thought back. Things started to fall apart when Sam was born. There was a lot of fighting, and Autumn used to sit in her room with the door closed and the pillow over her head. Eventually her parents divorced, and her father moved to Minneapolis, several hours away. She hadn't seen him in a long time.

Autumn's mother worked two jobs, trying to keep the family going. Autumn had watched as her outgoing, always-smiling mother became unhappy and sometimes mean. She expected Autumn to do all the chores around the house and help care for her little brother. It left little time for anything else. Autumn didn't mind it, though.

At least that's what she told herself.

As they pulled into the driveway of their little brown house, Autumn glanced out the passenger window of the car and noticed the leaves were starting to change color on her favorite oak tree.

She had been born in the early morning hours of October seventeenth, and her father gave her the name "Autumn Dawn." The day she was born, he had gone to the hospital nursery and unwrapped her hospital blanket to put her into a red-and-yellow one with Native designs. Aunt Jessie had made it for her, and Autumn still slept with it on her bed.

Autumn was jolted back to reality as her mother put the car in park and grabbed four bags of groceries from the trunk. She started to take them into the house, ignoring the fact Sam was still in the back seat. He started to fuss again, and Autumn slowly took her little brother out of the car, wondering why her mother had taken such a big shopping trip. She grabbed her backpack off the seat and shoved it over her other shoulder. Then she smiled and pushed Sam's curly black hair out of his face as he snuggled his plump body into his big sister's arms and yawned. He laid his head on her shoulder and watched his mother fumble with the keys to open the door to the house.

The house was small, with only two bedrooms. Autumn had a room to herself before Sam came along.

She headed to her bedroom now, gently settling Sam into his crib by the window. He fussed a minute, and Autumn gave him his pacifier. He sucked it eagerly and then closed his eyes.

She quietly dropped her book bag in the wooden chair by her dresser and sat on her bed to kick off her red moccasins. All the other kids in school wore tennis shoes, but she preferred these. They were comfortable, and her father had worn a pair just like them on the weekends. Wearing them helped her feel closer to him somehow.

"Autumn, can you come in here, please?"

Sighing, Autumn got up and headed for the kitchen. Her mother was sitting at the table with a cup of tea in front of her. She gestured to a chair, and Autumn reluctantly sat in it. Her mother looked serious, and Autumn wondered what was up.

For a moment, no one spoke, and then her mother sighed.

"I just called your aunt and asked her to come and stay with us for a while."

"What? Why?"

Autumn's mother sighed again. "I'm having a hard time with things right now," she admitted reluctantly. "I need some help. Jessie's apartment building is getting renovated over the next couple of months. She's anxious to get away from the noise and mess."

"What did she say?"

"She'll be here at the end of the week."

"Where is she going to sleep?"

Autumn's mother studied the contents of her cup. "I'm going to move Sam in with me. Jessie can room with you."

Autumn didn't know what to say. She didn't want Aunt Jessie moving in with them. It was bad enough sharing a room with a baby, but at least she had a little privacy at night when he was asleep. Now she would have no privacy at all. And on top of that, Autumn was having trouble with her schoolwork. She studied when she could, but she just couldn't seem to understand the material. She was starting to get notes sent home, which she had so far managed to hide from her mother. Aunt Jessie would surely pick up on the homework situation and then her mother would find out.

"Autumn?"

Autumn sighed. Maybe Aunt Jessie could help with the bills that were piling up. She'd seen her mother sitting at the kitchen table one night trying to decide which bills to pay and which to put back in the little box she kept them in. Autumn had felt helpless watching her mother try to cope with everything. She did her best to help, but she felt that nothing she did was ever good enough in her mother's eyes.

She glanced up to see her mother waiting for her to say something.

"Okay," she answered with a nod.

Her mother got up to put her cup away. "I thought we could start rearranging your room tonight. I can pull the crib into my room so Sam can start getting used to sleeping in there. That will also give you a little privacy before your aunt comes. I know how important that is to you."

Autumn's eyes shot up in surprise. She didn't think her mother had noticed that.

"I'm sorry to do this, but it's only for a little while," her mother went on. "I hate having someone else living here at the house. But it's been really hard to manage things since your father left."

"I know."

Autumn got up and pushed her chair in.

"Go start on your homework now," her mother added, and Autumn nodded.

"All right."

Heading back to her bedroom, Autumn grabbed her homework out of the backpack and went into the living room. Dropping her books on the coffee table, she turned on the TV and settled back on the couch.

"Autumn Dawn, turn off that TV and get some work done," said her mother from the kitchen.

As the TV went off and the books opened to display her homework for the night, Autumn wondered why she bothered looking at it. Half the time she didn't understand the questions, and the other half of the time the answers she wrote down were wrong or misspelled. She also hated to read out loud. She was a slow reader and sometimes mispronounced words. Some of the kids made fun of her, making jokes about her when they thought she couldn't hear them. She didn't understand why she couldn't learn as easily as everybody else. Maybe she was stupid, like Sydney said.

"Do you want some help?"

Autumn looked up to see her mother drying her hands on a dish towel.

"What?"

"You haven't started. Do you want some help with your homework? I have some time while your brother is sleeping." Her mother glanced down at the book on the table. "History, huh? We could read the questions together, and you can write down the answers."

Autumn shut the book. "Uh, no. I can handle it, Mom."

"Well, okay. But no TV until your homework is done."

"I know."

As her mother left the room, Autumn opened her book again. She started to read the chapter, but some of the words made no sense to her. She pulled out a sheet of paper and wrote her name at the top. It was going to be a long night, and it wouldn't include the TV.

A New Roommate

Autumn stood in the doorway holding her little brother while her mother silently helped Jessie Little Wolf into the house with her bags. Her aunt looked a lot like Autumn, with dark hair and dark brown eyes. Her black hair ran straight down to her waist, and she wore a T-shirt, ripped jean shorts, and flip-flops. She was twenty-eight and the youngest child of four, with Autumn's father being the oldest.

Autumn had her mother's nose, but that was about it. Everyone said she was the spitting image of her father, and apparently so was Jessie.

Her aunt didn't have much with her, and Autumn wondered why. She knew very little about her except that she lived in Minneapolis, and Autumn guessed that was why her father moved there.

"Hi, Autumn. I hear we're going to be roomies." Jessie reached over and kissed Sam's forehead. "I can't wait to play with you later, little guy."

Autumn set Sam down by his toys in the living room and showed her aunt to the room they would be sharing. Autumn's mother had bought a cot from a secondhand store and set it up for Jessie.

Sitting on her bed, which had now been moved to the other side of the room, Autumn watched her aunt pull a pillow, blanket, and some clothes out of a duffel bag.

"What's in the other bag?" Autumn asked. "Makeup?"

Jessie laughed. "No way. I never wear that stuff." She grabbed the bag off the floor and unzipped it. Out came a little loom, a box of beads, and some feathers. There was also some type of brown thread and large needles, among many other odds and ends.

"What's all that stuff for?" Autumn asked, reaching out to pick up the box of colorful beads.

"These are my craft supplies," said Jessie. "I'm working on several projects at the moment."

"Do you sew?" asked Autumn, eyeing the needles.

"Yes, among other things. Do you?"

Autumn shook her head and put the beads back in the pile. "I could have taken that class in school, but I took woodshop instead."

"Why?"

"There were more boys in that class."

Jessie laughed as Autumn grinned and added, "I made a wooden shelf for Mom. She hangs her keys on it."

"Well, I know nothing about woodcraft, but I do know how to sew. I could teach you while I'm here."

"Oh, I don't know . . . don't have much interest in that sort of stuff."

"Your father used to sew," remarked Jessie, putting her clothes in the little brown dresser she was going to share with Autumn.

"What? No way. He's a guy."

"Our mother taught us. She thought it was a useful skill for anyone to know. Your father did beadwork as well. He did beautiful work." She turned to look at Autumn. "Did he ever show you any of it?"

"No. I never saw him do anything like that. He was always working. Mom used to say he was the most hardworking man she ever knew."

"It's important in our culture for a man to take care of his family." Jessie hesitated and then added, "I know that sounds hard to believe since your father left you guys."

Autumn shrugged, picking some lint off her bedspread. There was silence for a moment, and then Jessie started taking something out of a small bag.

"What are those?" asked Autumn, eyeing the brass bells.

"These are jingles."

Autumn laughed. "Like jingle bells?"

Jessie grinned. "Something like that. They are sewn onto Jingle Dresses."

"We're doing a play in school called that."

"That's awesome. Are you going to try out?"

Autumn shook her head.

"Why?"

When Autumn didn't answer, Jessie sighed.

"Is it because you can't say your s's correctly?"

Autumn colored and slipped off the bed, heading for the door. She didn't want to talk about that.

"Well, I need to go make dinner . . ."

"You're making dinner?"

"Yes."

"Not your mother?"

"She's tired. I always make dinner."

"I see. Do you want some help?"

Autumn shrugged and then shook her head.

"I can do it."

Jessie smiled. "I know that. I was just volunteering to help out. That's why I'm here, you know."

"I know."

Jessie watched her leave and then sighed.

Tom certainly had an interesting daughter. She wondered again what had happened to the marriage that would convince him to move several hours away from his family. She saw him once in awhile, but he was closed-mouthed about the whole thing.

She didn't know Autumn's mom, Melissa, very well, but had been willing to help out when she called. This was her brother's family, and she would do what she could to make sure they were provided for.

Jessie got up and headed out the bedroom door. It was strange, but Melissa didn't seem to want her here even though she had asked her to come. And from what she had seen in the short time she'd been there, Autumn took care of almost everything around the house.

Well, she was here to help, and she was going to start now.

She entered the kitchen and saw Autumn doing the dishes and Melissa holding the squirming Sam on her hip while trying to wash down the little table. Jessie reached over to grab Sam, but he struggled against leaving his mother.

"He doesn't like anyone else to hold him," Melissa said, and Jessie smiled.

"If I am going to be of any help around here, I think it's time he gets used to it," she stated, reaching out and taking him.

Sam wailed and threw the best two-year-old tantrum Autumn had ever seen, but Jessie held on to him firmly, cooing into his ear. Melissa continued to clean the table, trying to ignore her son's screams. Eventually he calmed down and stuck his thumb in his mouth. Jessie took him into the living room and sat him on the couch next to her. He sniffled for a few moments and then smiled when he saw the toy she had in her hand.

Autumn peeked in on them a few minutes later and saw him playing happily on the floor next to Jessie. She looked back to give her mom a smile, which her mother ignored. Autumn sighed and went back to work.

Caught!

Autumn was slowly walking home from school. Her mother had called to say she had car trouble and Autumn was to walk home. Secretly, Autumn was glad.

She never had time alone anymore. With Aunt Jessie there, the little house seemed overcrowded, so Autumn was looking forward to the walk home no matter how cold it was outside.

She pulled her purple jacket around her. Looking up, she saw gray clouds and wondered if it was going to rain. It could snow, reasoned Autumn. It wasn't unheard of to get snow in October.

When she was little, she remembered trick-or-treating with a snowsuit on. She was very unhappy because it covered up the Cinderella costume she had underneath. At least people could still see the crown, her mother had said. It made her look like a princess, her father had added with that smile he saved just for her.

Autumn sighed and looked down at the pavement beneath her feet. She sure missed him.

Clutching her backpack strap, she wondered how long she could keep the letters from her teacher away from her mother. Today's letter was safely stashed away in the pocket of her jeans. This one asked her mother why she hadn't responded to the several that had already been sent home. It also asked for a meeting between Autumn, her mother, and her teacher. Autumn couldn't let that happen.

Glancing up, Autumn noticed a trash barrel outside the gas station. Autumn headed for it as she pulled out the note from her teacher.

"Autumn?"

Autumn froze and then spun around, clutching the note in her hand tightly. Her aunt had pulled up to the gas station and was getting out of the car.

"What are you doing at the gas station?" Jessie asked, walking over to her.

"I'm . . . uh . . . going to get a can of pop," Autumn replied, slowly shoving the hand with the note in it inside her pocket. "What are you doing here?"

"A friend of mine works here. We graduated from high school together. I was dropping in to say hello. What's that in your pocket?"

"Huh?"

"You just put something in your pocket."

"I did?"

"Let me see it, Autumn."

"Why?"

"Because it's something you don't want me to see. That makes it important."

Autumn shoved her hand inside her pocket and pulled out the now-crumpled piece of paper. "It's nothing. Just a note."

Jessie took it from her and read it. Then she glanced at Autumn and gave it back to her. "Since I'm here, I'll drive you home. It's getting colder by the minute. Do you want to get the pop first?"

Autumn shook her head and slowly followed her aunt to the car. She settled into the seat and clicked her seat belt.

"How many notes have been sent home?"

Autumn sighed. She guessed Aunt Jessie wasn't going to let this go like she'd hoped.

"A few," she replied, looking out the window.

"What's going on at school?"

"Nothing."

"Nothing?"

"I don't want to talk about it."

"Not to me, you mean?"

"Not to anyone, I mean."

They rode in silence for a few minutes, and then Jessie said, "Tell me what's been happening, and I won't tell your mother."

Autumn studied her aunt for a moment. "Really? Can you do that?"

"I probably shouldn't, and if someone is hurting you in any way, all bets are off. If not, maybe I can help you. Give me a chance. I'm not as dumb as I look."

She grinned, and Autumn couldn't help but grin back. Then she sighed. "I'm having trouble with my schoolwork."

"In what way?"

"I can't really explain it. I understand it when the teacher talks about it in class, but then when I see it in my book, it doesn't look the same as she explained it. It's very confusing."

"I see."

"You do?"

"Nope."

"Then why did you say you did?"

"I was trying to make you feel better."

Autumn laughed, and Jessie added, "Show me your homework when we get home, and I will see what I can do."

"Okay."

Pulling into the driveway, Jessie removed a sleeping Sam from his car seat and headed for the house. Autumn grabbed her book bag and followed her. She set her books on the kitchen table and sat down.

"How'd you get Sam to fall asleep in the car?" she asked her aunt.

Jessie set Sam in his crib and shut the door behind her. "Magic."

"Very funny. How'd you do it? Mom can never calm him down. He hates that car seat."

"I find if I'm calm, it makes others calm. Your mom doesn't have a calm mind."

"How do you stay calm when a baby is screaming and crying?"

"I take a deep breath and speak quietly," Jessie answered. "If you whisper, the other person stops what they are doing to hear what you have to say. When you have their attention, then you can distract them."

"How did you learn to do that?"

"My mom taught me." Jessie paused for a moment and then walked over to the kitchen table and sat down. "Did your dad ever talk about your grandparents?"

"Some."

"What did he say?"

"He told me some stories about how things were when he was growing up. You know, stuff like that."

"I see. Well, let's open the books and see what kind of homework you have."

Autumn pulled all her books out of her bag and laid them out in front of her. "I have history homework and math."

Jessie took the history book and started looking over the chapter. It was a long one that included facts about the Battle of the Little Bighorn.

"Remind me someday to tell you about this war from a Native American point of view," commented Jessie, setting the book in front of Autumn.

"You mean the book is wrong?"

"It's one-sided," said Jessie. "There are two sides to any conflict. Okay, read your first question out loud."

Autumn didn't want to. She couldn't read very well, and she didn't want to appear stupid in front of her aunt. "How about if you read the question, and I look for the answer?" she asked. "It will go faster then." She grabbed the book and pushed the homework sheet in front of her aunt.

Jessie watched her for a moment and then looked down at the paper. "Okay, then. Let's see . . . The Battle of . . . uh . . . Autumn, can you help me with this word, please?"

Autumn glanced at her aunt in surprise. "Really?"

"Yes, really. It's right here."

Autumn looked down at the page. "Title. The word is 'title.'"

"Thank you. The Battle of Title Bighorn was—"

"You mean Battle of *Little* Bighorn."

Jessie smiled. "You just told me the word was 'title.'"

Autumn shifted in her seat and pushed her hair out of her eyes. "I must have read it wrong. I just glanced at it really quick."

"Okay, so the question is, What year did it happen?"

Autumn flipped through her book, scanning the pages. When she thought she had found the answer, she replied, "1867."

Jessie pulled the book over to her to find where Autumn had found the answer. "You mean 1876."

Autumn looked down on the page again. It looked like 1867 to her.

"Autumn, show me where you found that answer."

Autumn pointed, and Jessie looked down to see 1876. Jessie set the worksheet down and sat back in her chair.

"Autumn, did you know your father was dyslexic?"

"What's that?"

"Let me tell you a story. When your father was a little boy, he was having trouble in school. No matter how much he studied, he almost always flunked tests. He had terrible grades, and Mom and Dad didn't know what to do with him. They could see him studying, but it didn't seem to matter. Dad wanted to write him off as being lazy or stupid, but Mom never gave up on him. One day, the teacher asked him to stand up and read a paragraph out of a book. As he fumbled through it, the teacher noticed he was making consistent mistakes. After class she pulled him aside and talked to him. Then she called Mom and Dad, and they went down to the school for a conference. They were told Tom probably had dyslexia."

"You still haven't told me what that is," said Autumn. "Was he sick?"

Jessie shook her head. "People who have this look at words and numbers on a page but see them differently than everyone else. They can be turned around or backwards. A *b* can become a *d*. For them, reading 'a drive to the park' might become 'the park drive to.'" Jessie stopped for a moment and then added, "And 'little' can become 'title,' and '1876' can become '1867.'"

Just then the phone rang. Jessie gave Autumn a smile and got up to answer it. "I'll be right back and we can talk about this some more."

Autumn watched her answer the phone and disappear into the other room. She looked down at her books again and then back to the doorway her aunt had disappeared through. She didn't know what to think. Did she really have dyslexia like her father? Did it run in the family? How come her mother never told her about her father's problem with reading?

A cry from her mother's room interrupted her thoughts. Sam was awake. Autumn got up and headed for the crib. Picking up her little brother, she tried to remember what Jessie had told her about staying calm. After Autumn stroked the baby's hair a few minutes and cooed words of comfort into his ear, he stopped crying and gave Autumn a watery smile. Autumn cuddled him close and gave him a kiss on the forehead. After a few more moments, Sam fell back to sleep and Autumn laid him back down in his crib.

Staring down at him, she wondered if Sam would have this dyslexia problem like his father. And if she herself really had this issue, she'd better learn how to deal with it. Autumn turned and headed for the living room. After all, someone was going to have to teach Sam.

A Welcome Ally

S itting in her room doing her homework, Autumn thought back to the teacher's meeting that she and Aunt Jessie had after school the day before. Jessie had explained that Autumn's mother was working and was unable to attend, so she sent Jessie in her place. The teacher seemed to be all right with that, even offering Jessie some coffee, which she declined.

Jessie had sat quietly listening as the teacher took out Autumn's homework from the past several weeks and pointed out the problems she had with it. After she was finished, Jessie leaned forward and asked the teacher if she had ever considered the idea that Autumn might be dyslexic. When the teacher replied that she had seen no indication that Autumn would need to be tested for something like that, Jessie remarked that it must hard to keep track of the work habits of all the thirty-two students she had in her class. "It's easy to miss," she had added with a smile, "especially if there are students who are acting up in class and need more attention on a daily basis than Autumn does."

After more discussion, it was decided that Autumn would be tested the following week. In the meantime, the teacher would be paying close attention to Autumn's work in class and the homework that was sent home every night. Jessie thanked the teacher for her time and took Autumn home, telling her she needed to let her mother know what was happening. The teacher had sent home forms that her mother would need to sign in order for the testing to be done. Autumn had reluctantly agreed. Jessie added that she would be glad to speak to her mother on her behalf. She would make sure her mother understood that this was a problem Autumn had thought she could handle herself, and that's why she wasn't told about it in the beginning.

When the meeting was over, Autumn went to her locker to grab a book she needed for her homework, while Jessie finished up with the teacher.

Autumn had started walking back down the hall when Sydney spied her and started walking her way.

"Get into trouble again, dummy?" she jeered, and Autumn's face flushed red. She held her book tighter and hurried down the hall toward the classroom Jessie was still in.

"You too stupid to answer?"

Sydney reached her before she got to the classroom and backed her up against a locker.

"Do you remember what I said about the play? I'm not going to see you there, right?"

Autumn bit her lip and said nothing.

Sydney pushed her against the locker hard, and Autumn dropped her book. She bent down to pick it up, but Sydney grabbed her arm.

"If I catch you there, I won't be happy," she hissed. "The play is my domain, understand? No one wants dummies like you there anyway." She laughed and let go of Autumn. "No one has any use for someone like you. Why do you think your father left? He probably hated how dumb his kids turned out to be."

"Autumn, are you ready to go?" asked Jessie, eyeing the two girls from down the hall. It was pretty easy to figure out what was happening between them, but Jessie said nothing as she motioned Autumn to her.

As Sydney took a step back, Jessie smiled at her.

"You look familiar. Are you Angie Goodwin's daughter?"

"Yes."

Jessie nodded. "We went to school together. You look just like her. How is she?"

"Fine," answered Sydney, feeling uncomfortable now. She knew Jessie had seen her and Autumn talking a moment ago . . . and the woman knew her mother.

Autumn walked down the hall toward her aunt, her gaze to the floor. She was embarrassed her aunt had seen what happened with Sydney.

Jessie gestured Sydney over to them as the teacher joined them in the doorway of the classroom. Sydney reluctantly walked over to them.

"Is there a problem?" the teacher asked, and Jessie shook her head.

"Nope. I was just saying hello to the daughter of an old classmate of mine."

"I see. Well, have a good day. Autumn, I will see you tomorrow."

The teacher smiled at Sydney and then walked back into the room, closing the door behind her. Jessie held her smile at Sydney until the woman was gone. Then she stepped away from the classroom door and pulled Sydney with her down the hall. Shocked, Autumn trailed behind her.

"Hey! Let go of me!" Sydney tried to pull away, but Jessie held tight. When they had reached the door, Jessie handed Autumn her keys.

"Go get in the car. I will be there in a minute."

"But . . ."

"Now, Autumn."

Autumn walked quickly down the hall, pushed the door open, and walked through it, leaving it ajar so she could see and hear what was happening. Jessie turned around and dropped Sydney's arm. Sydney immediately started to back away and turned to walk quickly down the hall. Jessie's words stopped her.

"If you don't turn around and face me, I will go immediately to speak with your mother. She still works at the gas station, right? She was one of my best friends. It might be time to pay her a visit."

Sydney started walking again, and Jessie added, "I understand the principal is still here." She started to walk slowly down the hall toward Sydney. "I am going to see that you get expelled."

Sydney slowed down but didn't turn around.

"For what?" Sydney asked. "I didn't do anything."

"Then why are you running away from me?"

"I . . . I thought you were going to hurt me."

"That's crap and you know it. This is your last chance to stop and talk to me or life is going to change as you know it."

Sydney stopped, not turning around. Jessie took her time getting to the girl. When she finally reached her, she circled around her.

"I saw what's happening between you and Autumn, and it's going to stop right now. This school has a no-tolerance policy for bullying. I'm going to have you expelled immediately."

"What? I didn't do anything wrong."

Jessie crossed her arms and gave Sydney a look.

"Well, you can't prove anything. It would be Autumn's word against mine." Sydney's chin went up. "And my father is president of the school board."

"Just think how proud he'll be when he finds out his daughter has been expelled for bullying someone," answered Jessie. "And for your information, Autumn told me nothing. It just so happens I heard you and saw what you were doing in the hall just now. You're lucky I didn't tell the teacher."

Sydney looked away but said nothing.

"Now, here's what you're going to do. Tomorrow, you're going to apologize to Autumn and then leave her alone. If I find out this has continued, there's going to be trouble. If and when Autumn shows up to audition for that play, you are going to say and do nothing. Do you understand? Because I can tell you right now, if this continues, you will spend the rest of the year being homeschooled. Have I made myself clear?"

"Aren't you bullying me right now?" challenged Sydney.

Jessie gave her a smile that didn't quite reach her eyes. "I'm giving you a reason to correct your behavior," she replied. "I am only trying to guide you. If you choose to continue on your current path, you now know what will happen."

When Sydney didn't respond, Jessie sighed. "What happens now is up to you. Why do you act like this toward other people? Think about it. Some self-reflection might be good for you."

Autumn saw her aunt was turning to leave and let the door shut. She turned around and walked quickly to the car. Jessie joined her a moment later.

"You're not above scolding," her aunt said. "I asked you to go wait in the car."

"I know. I'm sorry."

Jessie shook her head and they left for home.

Autumn shook herself out of her thoughts and went back to her homework. She wondered if the talk with Jessie would really change anything where Sydney was concerned. It might make things worse, and she was a little afraid.

She managed to get most of her math problems finished by the time her mother came home from work that night. She stayed in her room because she could hear her mother and Jessie talking in the kitchen. In the beginning, her mother was very angry Jessie had butted in where she didn't belong. Jessie had quietly replied that she had come to help in any way possible, and that included any issues concerning Sam and Autumn. Eventually her mother calmed down and realized Jessie only had Autumn's best interests at heart. She signed the paperwork for Autumn to return to her teacher.

"Autumn . . . I see you are busy with your homework, but I would like to speak to you."

Autumn looked up from her book to see her mother standing in the doorway. The house was quiet, and Autumn knew they were alone. Jessie had taken Sam out in his stroller for a walk around the block. Autumn had wondered about that. It seemed a little too chilly for that sort of thing. Now she knew why.

Sitting up in her bed, she watched her mother sit down on Jessie's bed.

"I wish you would have told me this was going on," she said.

"I'm sorry," Autumn mumbled, looking down at the bed. She started to pick the lint off her bedspread.

"Well, anyway, I just wanted you to know I didn't know your dad was dyslexic until Aunt Jessie told me yesterday."

"Oh."

"Your father never mentioned it. I had a hard time believing it myself until Jessie explained that he had years to master a way to deal with it. He still messed things up once in awhile, but I chalked it up to him reading something too fast or not paying attention." She sighed. "I feel like I should have noticed that something was wrong with regard to you."

"No . . . there's no way you could have known. I worked really hard to cover it up."

"Why would you do that?"

"I thought if I ignored it, it would go away or fix itself."

"Autumn, you can't hide from your problems. You have to face them head on. Jessie mentioned a note from your teacher."

Autumn grimaced. "There were several. I threw them away. I didn't want to get yelled at." When her mother's eyes narrowed, Autumn sighed and her bottom lip started to tremble. She cleared her throat.

"I felt so stupid," she whispered. "I couldn't do the work like everyone else."

"How did you get all the way to eighth grade without anyone catching this problem? At all the teacher conferences, I was told you just didn't apply yourself. They said you did all right in class, but you didn't turn your homework in."

Autumn shrugged. "Most days I could figure out enough of it to at least pass a test or get a passing grade on my homework," she said. "If I couldn't figure something out, I just didn't do it."

Autumn's mother went silent for a moment and then shook her head. "And I've been so unhappy about your father leaving, I couldn't see what was going on around me."

"It's okay, Mom."

"No, it's not, but it is what it is." She reached out and touched Autumn on the arm.

"I would like you to spend some more time with your aunt Jessie."

"Why?"

"I know what a mess I've been. I need some time to sort things out, I guess. In the meantime, Jessie is a good person. She's your dad's sister and knows about the Ojibwa side of your family."

"Oh."

"Don't you want to know about your Native American heritage?"

Autumn gave it some thought and then replied with a shrug. "I guess so. I'm not sure I want to learn how to sew and stuff like that, though."

"Well, how about beadwork? Or maybe learning how to make traditional foods?"

"Isn't beadwork sewing? Well, maybe the food part. I like to eat," Autumn replied with a grin.

Her mother laughed, and Autumn smiled at her. She hadn't heard that sound in a long time.

"Yes, I know you do," replied her mother. "You know, your dad used to sew. He made me a pair of moccasins the first year we were together. I used to wear them everywhere."

"I didn't know that. Why don't you wear them anymore?"

"They make me sad now."

"Do you miss Dad?" Autumn asked. "I know you guys used to fight all the time . . ."

"Yes, we did," agreed her mother. "But there was a lot of love there too."

"So what happened then? Why did he leave?" Autumn leaned back and looked away. "Things aren't the same with him gone."

"That's not such a bad thing," her mother pointed out. "There's not so much yelling now."

"I miss him," said Autumn. "Is he going to come back and see us soon?"

"I don't know," replied Autumn's mother quietly. "Now that things have calmed down some, I was hoping he would want to talk." She shook her head. "But I guess not."

"Maybe he doesn't know you want to."

"That could be." Her mother stood up and pushed her blonde hair behind her ears. Autumn knew by that gesture that the conversation was over.

"I'm going to go do some laundry," she said, glancing over at Autumn one last time. "Can you start dinner?"

Autumn nodded and watched her mother leave. She knew her mother was still upset about the divorce. She didn't know why her father didn't want to talk to any of them. No one had heard from him in ages. Autumn felt so bad. She used to be Daddy's girl. Now she felt like she was no one special.

She thought about Aunt Jessie. Maybe it would be nice to get to know her better. She was curious about her father's side of the family, and Jessie could tell her about them.

She wondered if Jessie was in contact with her father. Maybe she would ask her after dinner. If he knew how badly her mother missed him, he might come for a visit, and then maybe things would get better around there.

She jumped off the bed and went into the kitchen to start dinner. She couldn't wait to talk to Jessie.

CHAPTER 5

Easier Said Than Done

After some testing at school and another parent-teacher conference that her mother attended this time, it was determined that Autumn was dyslexic. An Individualized Education Plan was set into place for her, and she went back to classes with a renewed sense of hope for her future.

Jessie was driving her nuts about the auditions for the play that were coming up. Autumn pretended not to care, but she secretly took a peek at the script that was on the drama teacher's desk. It was a wonderful story, and Autumn loved it right away. She could just picture herself as the main character, but she knew there were a lot of lines to memorize. In the past, she would have run away as fast as she could from the idea of being in a play. But now she wondered if she could do it.

"Everyone learns things differently," her aunt had told her the other day. "In some cases, it doesn't matter how you get from point A to point B; it just matters that you get there," she had said.

Jessie had been picking her up after school once in awhile and taking her out for ice cream or to go shopping. The two were getting close, and Autumn was glad to have someone around to talk to. Before Jessie came to live with them, Autumn didn't have much time for herself. With Jessie living with them, she was able to take a walk after school, do her homework earlier, and even watch TV after supper.

Today Jessie was picking her up, and they were going to head out to the fabric store to buy some leather. Autumn was going to make her first pair of moccasins.

"What color leather do you want to use?" asked Jessie, pulling into the parking lot of the store.

"Well, I have a pair of red ones now," Autumn answered. "But they are getting a little too small. You know, I really don't like sewing."

"Well, just try it once and see what you think. What are you going to use them for?"

"What do you mean?"

"Are you going to wear them every day? Are you going to dance in them?"

"Dance in them?" Autumn laughed. "I don't think so."

Jessie locked the car doors, and they headed to the store's entrance. "I'm not talking about that sort of dancing. Haven't you ever been to a pow wow?"

"Yes, when I was little. Mom doesn't go to them anymore. She says she feels funny being there without Dad."

"Did you dance there?"

"No."

"If you learn the Jingle Dress dance, maybe you could try out for the play."

"I'm not trying out."

"Why?"

Autumn looked away, tucking her hair behind her ear. "I don't talk right."

"You are doing so much better with your dyslexia."

"No, I mean my . . ." Autumn's voice trailed off and she looked down at the ground.

Jessie pulled her to the side of the building next to the door and looked down at her.

"Has anyone been teasing you? I mean, have you had problems with Sydney?"

Autumn shook her head. "No, but no one comes near me anymore, either." She gave her aunt a little smile. "I think they are afraid of you."

Jessie shook her head. "Well, I didn't mean for that to happen."

"It's okay."

"No, it's not." She thought for a moment. "Are you concerned about your speech issues?"

Autumn nodded.

"Haven't you been working with your speech therapist?"

"Yes, but it's not getting any better."

"These things take time."

"I don't have time. Auditions are in a couple of weeks."

"Autumn, everyone knows you have this issue. It shouldn't stop you from trying new things."

"It does."

"But it shouldn't."

"It's embarrassing."

"I know it is." Jessie sighed and shoved her hands in her jean pockets. "You know, some of us carry our carry our burdens on the inside and some of us on the outside."

"Huh?"

Jessie smiled. "With some people you can tell they have a problem. Maybe they walk with crutches or a cane. Those people carry their problems on the outside. You are having speech issues. People can't tell you are different unless you speak. You carry your problems on the inside."

"So what's your point?"

"My point is this problem may never go away. You just have to learn to live with it the best you can. If you are confident, others will see you that way."

"That's easier said than done."

"I know."

"And people have made fun of me because of the way I talk. Why would I want to put myself out there for that?"

Jessie took Autumn's hand and looked into her eyes.

"Your grandmother used to tell me, 'If people are trying to bring you down, it only means one thing. You already are above them.'"

"Oh, I don't know about that."

"You are not alone, Autumn Dawn. I am here. And your mother." Jessie saw the skeptical way Autumn was looking at her and she smiled.

"Your mother is a little lost right now, but she will come back to us. I told her something the other day that I think will help you too."

"What is it?"

"It's an Ojibwa proverb that goes like this: 'Sometimes I go about pitying myself, and all the while I am being carried across the sky by beautiful clouds.'"

"And just what are you saying? This is all my fault because I'm feeling sorry for myself?"

Jessie shook her head and started walking back to the front door of the store. Autumn trailed behind her.

"The proverb means you are never alone," replied Jessie. "When you feel bad about yourself, look around you and see that you have support to get through it."

"So, you are the beautiful cloud?"

Jessie laughed. "Your father used to call me that."

Autumn grinned and linked her arm with Jessie's.

"Well, if you are already carrying Dad, then I guess I could hop on too," she said with a smile. "Let's go get some white leather."

"White?"

"Yup. I like that color."

"Okay then. Let's go."

Together they went into the store and bought the needed items for the moccasins. Then they headed home to make supper.

Autumn could tell right away there was a problem when they entered the house. There was a pot of noodles on the stove overflowing, and Sam was wailing on the living room floor. Her mother was nowhere to be found.

Jessie's look was grim as she went over and picked up Sam. Autumn went into the kitchen, turned off the stove, and moved the pot off the burner. Then she walked over to her mother's bedroom and tentatively knocked on the closed door.

"Mom?"

"What?"

"What are you doing?"

"That's none of your business. Go away!"

Autumn looked over at Sam still screaming and the mess in the kitchen. She had been having a wonderful time with her aunt and now she had to come home to this. Her mother had ruined things again. Her eyes narrowed, and this time she couldn't stop the angry words from coming out of her mouth.

"You need to get out here and take care of things," she shouted at the closed door. "I'm tired of doing everything around here!"

The door whipped open and she stood face to face with her mother.

"What did you just say to me?" asked her mother, eyes narrowing.

"You need to get over yourself," said Autumn, hands on her hips. "So Dad left you. We are still here. You are our mother. Start taking care of us. What's wrong with you that you dump everything on me? I shouldn't have to do everything."

Autumn's head whipped back from the slap her mother gave her.

Autumn sucked in a breath as tears rolled down her face.

"I hate you," she whispered. Before Jessie could stop her, she shoved her mother back in the room and pulled the door shut hard.

"Stay in there," Autumn yelled. "No one wants you out here anyway."

Her mother managed to fling the door open as Autumn ran out of the house, leaving the outside door open. Autumn's mother took a few steps toward the door and Jessie caught her arm. She pushed her off, turning on her.

"You! You've filled her head with all this. She never used to talk to me that way."

Jessie shook her head sadly. "You have made her that way, Melissa," she answered.

When Melissa took a step toward her, Jessie put up a hand.

"Are you really going to hit me with your son in my arms?"

Melissa gritted her teeth and, with a growl, marched back into the bedroom and slammed the door. Jessie sighed and worked on quieting down the toddler in her arms.

A few moments later, Jessie could hear sobbing coming from Melissa's bedroom, and she took a step toward it. She stopped and glanced back at the outside door, which was still swinging in the breeze.

She turned around and headed for it. Autumn needed her more. She just hoped she could find her.

Nothing Is Solved by Running Away

Autumn sat hunched over in a big brown wooden fort at the playground down the block from her house. There were several steps leading up to the platform where she was hiding, and she huddled against one of the four enclosed walls with her eyes closed.

She was never going home. She hated it there and was tired of her mother. Jessie was there now, she reasoned, and she could handle things while her mother fell apart.

Starting to shiver, she pulled her arms out of her sweatshirt and hugged herself for warmth. She didn't know what to do now that she had left. She had no food or money and nowhere to go. She started to cry softly, afraid someone would hear her and try to take her back home . . . or worse, try to hurt her in some way.

Eventually she fell asleep. She woke up several hours later when she heard someone calling her name. It was her mother.

"Autumn! Can you hear me?"

Autumn didn't know what to do. She was torn between staying where she was and answering the frantic call of her mother. She bit her lip and stayed put.

Autumn's mother started to cry as she called out again.

"Autumn, please. If you can hear me, answer me."

Autumn stayed where she was and didn't answer.

Autumn's mother sat down on the platform below Autumn and sighed.

"She's gone. I'll never find her. She could be anywhere. What was I thinking hitting her like that? I've never hit anyone in all my life. But I'm so angry. I'm angry Tom left, I have no money even though I'm working two jobs, and I have no time for myself. I just don't know what to do."

She started crying again, and Autumn bit her lip. She wanted to run down the stairs and fling herself into her mother's arms, but she couldn't be sure her mother wouldn't hit her again. Her cheek still stung from the hard slap she had given her. And what if she got mad at her for hiding right next to her and not coming out right away? No, she didn't trust her. She had to stay hidden.

All was silent after a few minutes, and Autumn wondered if her mother had left. She reached up and peered out through a little space between the wood and saw her aunt coming toward them. She quickly dropped back down and waited.

"No sign of her over there," Jessie said. "Come on. We need to take Sam home and call the police."

"The police!" Autumn mouthed quietly. She never considered they would have to do that. She shifted quietly in her place in the fort.

"The police? Why would we do that?" asked her mother.

"Melissa, you're not thinking clearly. It's getting dark out here. Then she'll be alone and possibly lost in the dark."

"Oh, no. You're right. I guess I thought we would have found her by now."

Autumn heard her mother get up from the platform.

"They're never going to find her," she said, starting to cry. "She could be long gone by now."

"I don't think so."

"You don't?"

"Nope. I think she's somewhere nearby."

"Really? Why do you think that?"

"She has no money, and she's probably getting hungry by now. I bet she heads home real soon. Maybe she's already there."

"Let's get back then."

Autumn heard her mother start to walk away.

"I'm right behind you," said Jessie.

There was a moment of silence, and then Jessie spoke up again.

"I saw you, Autumn, peeking out from the fort. It's time to go home. Nothing can be solved by running away."

Autumn dropped her face in her hands and didn't answer.

"Okay, Autumn. I'm heading home now. If you choose to come back, I'll make sure your mother doesn't hit you again."

Autumn heard her turn and walk away. She sat for several minutes trying to decide what to do. Then, realizing again she had no food or money, she stood up slowly.

Her legs felt cramped, and for a moment she just stood there. She could barely see the walls now. It was time to go.

Autumn crawled down from the fort and started walking home. She was several blocks away and needed to hurry, as the light was starting to fade. She hesitated outside her house, then opened the door and stepped inside her living room.

Jessie had told Melissa that she saw Autumn at the playground and had talked to her. Melissa wanted to run back to the playground, but Jessie had told her to wait. It had to be Autumn's decision to return, and as hard as that was to hear, Melissa knew she was right. If she went barging down there, she could scare her daughter, and Autumn might run away where she'd never find her. They decided to give Autumn an hour before they called the police. It was the longest hour of Melissa's life, and a great lesson in trust.

Autumn stood just inside the door, unsure of what reception she would get from her mother. Melissa stayed on the couch, and Jessie stood by the picture window watching. She would protect Autumn at all costs, but she was pretty sure she wouldn't need to.

Mother and daughter stood staring at each other, and for a moment no one spoke. Then Autumn closed the door behind her and walked into the room. She glanced at her mother and then at her aunt before walking across the room and disappearing into her bedroom, shutting the door. Melissa went to stand up, but Jessie motioned her to stay still.

"But . . ."

Jessie shook her head, and Melissa went still again.

A little while later, Melissa put Sam to bed. She paused just outside Autumn's bedroom door.

Jessie saw the worried look on Melissa's face and got up and went to her in the hall. She nodded, and together they entered Autumn's bedroom.

She was curled up facing the wall, with her back to the two women. Melissa sighed and sat down on Jessie's bed. Jessie remained standing but quietly shut the door behind them.

Melissa glanced at Jessie, who nodded, and she turned back to speak to Autumn.

"I'm so sorry, Autumn. You are the most precious thing to me, and I hurt you."

There was no response, and Melissa frowned, glancing up at Jessie again. Jessie gestured that she should continue, and Melissa turned back to her daughter reluctantly. She didn't know what to say.

Jessie patted the place over her heart and nodded, and Melissa spoke again.

"I'm in a lot of pain because your dad left us," she said, shifting on the bed. "I guess I took it out on you. I made you do everything around here while I felt sorry for myself. That was wrong, and I'm sorry for that."

She hesitated and then went on.

"I just don't know what to do anymore. I can't seem to move on. Your dad has been gone for a while now, and I'm stuck in this black hole. I wish . . ."

Her voice trailed off and then she went silent. Autumn turned over to stare at her mother.

"What do you wish?" she asked softly, and tears filled her mother's eyes.

"I wish so many things," she whispered. "I wish I was a better mother. I wish I could handle all this better. I wish I hadn't hit you." Tears fell from her eyes, and she looked down at the floor, ashamed now.

"I'm so sorry," she said, and Autumn got up and wrapped her arms around her.

"Me too," she said. "I shouldn't have said all those things to you."

"No, you were right. Everything you said was true," replied her mother, wiping her tears away. "I just didn't want to hear them."

Autumn closed her eyes and pulled her mother closer. Her mother buried her face in Autumn's hair.

"You look so much like your father," she said. "Every time I look at you I see him."

Autumn opened her eyes to see Jessie watching her. She nodded at Autumn, and put a hand to her heart. Then she turned and quietly left the room.

The Jingle Dress

The following week, things were going better at home and at school. Jessie was in the living room playing with Sam when Autumn came home on Friday. She patted the place beside her on the floor.

"Come talk with me," said Jessie. "I feel like it's been forever since we had some girl talk."

Autumn set her book bag down and plopped herself on the floor next to Sam. He smiled and reached out a chubby hand to give her a toy dinosaur.

"I am so glad it's Friday," said Autumn, reaching out and taking the toy. "I have no homework, and I plan to sleep in tomorrow."

"So that's your plan for the whole weekend?" teased Jessie. "You're going to sleep your life away?"

Autumn laughed and shook her head. "No, I'll just sleep in a few hours on Saturday."

"And then what?"

"I haven't figured that out yet."

"I have a suggestion."

"What?"

"How would you like to help me sew some beadwork on something?"

Autumn shook her head. "I don't sew very well."

"You don't sew very well *yet*," corrected Jessie. "You just need practice."

"Oh, I don't know . . ."

"Come on," replied Jessie, picking up a yawning Sam. "It will be fun."

She stood up and smiled down at Autumn.

"I'll put your brother to bed for his nap, and you and I will go in and take a look at what has to be done."

"Okay. I guess so."

Autumn stood up and headed to her bedroom. Jessie joined her a moment later after shutting Sam's door.

Jessie went to her dresser drawer and pulled out a piece of beadwork she had finished. It was a red flower with green leaves. Autumn thought it was beautiful and told her aunt so.

Jessie smiled. "Thanks. Now hang on while I get the garment I'm working on."

She headed for the closet, humming a little, and Autumn smiled in spite of herself. When Jessie turned around, Autumn saw a simple red dress with long sleeves. It was made out of cotton. It didn't look like much, but she wasn't about to say that and hurt her aunt's feelings.

Jessie saw her skeptical look and chuckled.

"It doesn't look like much right now, but when I get it all done, it will be beautiful."

"It looks a little short for you," replied Autumn.

Jessie nodded. "It is." She gave Autumn a little smile. "I'm making it for you."

"Me?"

"Yes. It's a Jingle Dress."

Autumn's breath caught in her throat. "A Jingle Dress? Like the one in the play at school? You know, the one I was going to try out for but changed my mind?"

"Yes."

"But why are you making it for me?"

"I thought maybe you would like to learn the dance."

"Me? Oh, I don't dance very well."

Jessie shrugged. "Every Native girl should have a dress to dance in. I will teach you the steps. They're easy."

"But why would I want to learn?" asked Autumn. "It's not like I can go to the school dance with these moves."

Jessie laughed. "Probably not. But they will come in handy when you do the school play."

Autumn sat down in her bed cross-legged and put her chin in her hands.

"I'm not trying out for the play."

"Why not?"

"Well, I can't say my s's and people laugh at me. And learning the script would take forever with my dyslexia."

"So?"

"So?"

"So what?"

"Well, it would be too hard for me . . ."

"Life is hard, Autumn. You can't be afraid to get out of your comfort zone once in awhile."

Autumn shook her head.

"Oh, come on. I will help you. So will your mother."

"She doesn't have the time."

"Yes, she does, and she would be so excited to see you in the play." Jessie stopped a moment to think and then added, "Maybe I could call your dad and see if he would like to come too."

"Really? Do you think he would?" Autumn sat up and slid off the bed, going over to her aunt. "I haven't seen him in ages." She glanced away a moment. "I . . . I thought maybe he didn't like me anymore."

"Oh, Autumn." Jessie sighed, putting the dress down on her bed. "This has nothing to do with you, honey. Your mom and dad are having some issues right now. Your father loves you very much."

"How do you know?"

"He told me when I called him last night."

"You talked to him last night? What did he say? Did he ask about me?"

"He did. I told him things were going better for you at school."

"He knew about that?" Autumn sat back down on the bed. "I bet he thinks I'm a real loser."

"Why on earth would he think that?"

"People only bully the weirdos."

"I was bullied, and I'm not weird." Seeing Autumn's frown, she added, "Well, not *that* weird."

Autumn grinned. "You were bullied?"

"Yes, and that's why I have no time for people like Sydney. She hasn't been bothering you, has she?"

Autumn shook her head.

"Good. Sometimes talking to bullies about their behavior makes it worse."

"I think you made an impression on her."

Jessie grinned. "I hope so." She walked over to pick up the dress again. "So . . . wanna help me get this finished?"

"I guess so," Autumn replied reluctantly. "But I'm not sure about the play."

"When are tryouts?"

"Next Tuesday."

Jessie nodded. "Well, in any case, let's get going on the dress. It all has to be hand sewn, you know. There are three hundred and sixty-five jingles to be sewn on there as well."

"Wow! I didn't know that. I don't know how I can help."

"I said I would teach you all that."

"What if I don't try out for the play?"

"Then I will take you to a pow wow."

"I do remember going to one of those when I was younger. I loved watching the pretty ladies in their regalia. They were so beautiful."

"And you will be, too, in your regalia."

Just then Sam started to cry, and with a sigh, Jessie put away her sewing.

Autumn smiled as she followed the older woman out of the room. For the first time in a long while, she had something to look forward to.

Learning
the Dance

Monday came along and Autumn nervously approached her teacher after school to ask her about auditioning for the play. Miss Jergens was directing the show this year.

"I think that's great that you want to audition," her teacher said. "I think you would do a wonderful job."

Autumn looked down at her feet. "What about my speech problems? I can't say an s right. And with my dyslexia, I will have problems reading the script and memorizing." She sighed. "Maybe I should just forget about it."

"Now, Autumn, you can do anything you set your mind to. I believe in you."

"You do?"

"Of course. I can spot talent, too. I bet there's a part for you in the play. Now, I want to see you at auditions tomorrow, okay?"

"Okay."

Autumn went home and told Aunt Jessie about her conversation with the teacher.

Aunt Jessie nodded. "See? You're the only one who doesn't think you can do it."

"I guess."

"Look how well you can sew, and you didn't know it. I bet you can act too. There's no limit to what you can do if you set your mind to it."

Autumn look down at the neat little stitches she was doing. Her aunt was working on sewing the jingles on the dress, and Autumn had sewn the beadwork on. The dress no longer looked plain. It was starting to look like the beautiful regalia that she had seen dancers wear. She was excited she, too, had something she could dance in when Jessie took her to a pow wow.

"I still don't know the dance," she reminded her aunt, and Jessie smiled.

"I will teach you tonight."

"Do you really think I can get the steps down?"

"Yes. It is a fairly simple dance, as long as you can feel the beat of the drums."

"Feel the beat?"

Jessie stopped sewing a moment and closed her eyes. "The drums are like a heartbeat—thump, thump, thump. If you close your eyes, you can almost feel it keeping time with your heart."

Autumn closed her eyes as Jessie talked. She could almost feel the rhythm of the drums echoing in her chest.

She opened her eyes and smiled. "Did Dad know how to do this dance?"

Jessie shook her head. "This is a dance for girls only. Do you know the story of the Jingle Dress?"

"No."

"The traditional way to do the dance is the dancers never cross their feet and they never dance backward. They also never complete a circle."

"I see."

"The footwork is light and bouncy too."

"So they jump around?"

Jessie laughed. "Not quite."

"So they move forward the whole time?"

"More or less. So let me tell you the story. Around the time of the First World War, a young Ojibwa girl became very sick. It was thought she might have had Spanish influenza. Her father was afraid she was going to die, so he looked for a vision that would save her. He had a dream in which he saw the dress and the instructions for how to sew it. In the dream he was told that the steps would need to be spring-like, keeping one foot on the ground at all times. He sewed the dress and then asked his daughter to dance in it. She kept dancing until she started to feel better and was no longer sick."

"Her father sewed the dress?"

"Yes."

"What happened after she got better?"

"Others were shown the dance, and eventually there became a Jingle Dress Dance Society." Jessie smiled. "You know, the dress represents the power of women and how we can help heal the spirits and health of our people."

"So, it's a healing dress?"

"Yes."

"Wow, that's awesome," replied Autumn. "All that from a dance?"

Jessie smiled and laid her sewing aside. "Let's go start supper. Your mom will be home soon."

"What are we having?"

"Turkey."

"We had turkey sandwiches last night."

"Well, we have leftovers. I'm going to make turkey and wild rice soup. Wild rice is something Ojibwa people harvest and sell."

"I know that. I live here on the reservation, you know."

Jessie grinned. "Yes, you do. Well, I picked some up this morning. Let's get supper started."

Autumn was deep in thought as she followed her aunt out of the room. This Jingle Dress had a lot more to it than she first thought. She hoped she could learn the steps and be able to perform the dance.

She walked by a family picture in the hall. She stopped, staring at it. If she could get the dress finished and learn the dance, maybe she could heal what's going on with her father and mother.

Humming now, she walked into the kitchen and got busy pulling out pans and the cutting board.

She just knew things were going to work out for the better for everybody.

The Dinner Guest

"T hat was wonderful, Autumn."

Autumn smiled at Miss Jergens. She had been able to look at the script ahead of time so she could figure out some of the words and had auditioned with only one mistake. When she made it, no one had laughed at her either.

"Thank you, Miss Jergens," she replied, handing the script back to her.

"The play will be cast by tomorrow," announced her teacher. "I will post the cast list on my door by lunchtime. Rehearsals will start next week. If you are cast, come and get your script from me tomorrow and start learning your lines. Any questions?"

Sydney raised her hand and was called upon.

"Is it true you wrote the script?"

"Yes, it is."

Autumn didn't know that, and when she glanced over at Miss Jergens, she saw she was smiling. Apparently she was excited they were going to perform a play she had written.

Autumn headed home after the auditions, thinking about her teacher. Her teacher had dressed up a little today, pulling her long black hair into a messy bun with soft curls framing her face. She had worn a pencil skirt and a royal-blue blouse with long sleeves. She was new, and this was her first school play. Autumn liked her and hoped she would be cast in the show.

Twenty minutes later, Autumn arrived home. Her mother was there.

"You're home early," said Autumn, pushing the front door shut.

"I called your father, and he is headed over here," replied Melissa. "I thought I should straighten up the house."

"Dad's coming here?"

"Yes."

"Why?"

"I thought it was about time we talked about some things."

"Like what?"

"That's between your father and me."

"You're not going to fight, are you?" Autumn set her book bag down on the chair. "Sam always cries when that happens."

"I know. And I don't know what will happen."

"Where's Jessie?"

"She went to get him. His car is in the shop again."

Her mother glanced over at the book bag. "Go put that in your room, please."

Autumn picked it up and headed for her room. She set the bag down next to her dresser and sat down on the bed.

Her father was coming home. She didn't know what to think. While she loved him a lot, she was also mad at him. Why didn't he visit or call? It was like he disappeared out of their lives and didn't care about them anymore. She wondered how her mother was able to get him to come back here.

She picked up her beadwork and ran her fingers lightly over the green beads. This turtle patch was going on one of her white moccasins. She had sewn the other one onto the left moccasin yesterday. She wondered what her father would say about her learning to do beadwork and sew.

It was almost suppertime when her father arrived with Aunt Jessie. Autumn was in the kitchen getting plates and silverware down from the cupboard when she heard his voice.

She set everything down on the counter and walked slowly into the living room. On the way, she patted her hair to be sure it had stayed in place.

Her hair had grown out some, and she had braided it and tied it off with a leather thong. Jessie said it made her look older, and Autumn had been pleased to hear that. She wondered what her father would think.

Tom walked into the house wondering what kind of reception he was going to get. Several months ago he had walked out and never returned. He hadn't called or visited since then. He sent his child support in regularly, but that was it. Melissa had hurt him so much, and there was still a lot of anger there. When she finally called and asked him to come and see the kids and talk with her about some things, he hadn't wanted to do it. It was only when she pointed out that his kids missed him that he changed his mind. Secretly he was ashamed for having abandoned his children and wouldn't blame Autumn if she didn't want to see him ever again. It wasn't her fault everything with her mother had gone sour.

Tom had Sam in his arms when Autumn walked into the room. Father and daughter stared at each other for a moment, neither speaking.

"I was just telling your dad about the play," said Jessie, gesturing for her to come and sit next to her on the couch.

Autumn moved to the couch and sat down. Her father watched her with his dark eyes.

"You're looking very grown up," he said. "I like the braid."

Autumn said nothing. She sighed and then looked away for a moment.

Her father tried again.

"So, tell me about this play you tried out for. What part do you hope to get?"

Autumn shrugged, and it wasn't until her mother caught her eye that she gave him a verbal answer.

"I will be happy with whatever part I get," she said, crossing her arms and leaning back on the couch. She looked away.

Jessie saw Autumn close off and tried to help.

"Tom, Autumn is learning to do beadwork and sew," she said.

"Really? That's great. I do beadwork as well. Have I ever shown you any of it?"

Autumn glanced over at her father and shook her head.

"I think I still have some of it here. Melissa, do you have any of my beadwork around here?"

"I . . . I have the moccasins you gave me when we were going out. You did beadwork on them, I think."

"Go get them and show Autumn." When she didn't move, Tom glanced over at her. "Please?" he added quietly.

Melissa got up and went into the bedroom. A moment later she came out with red moccasins.

Autumn gasped. They were just like hers, only bigger.

Autumn took them from her mother and marveled at the carefully placed beads that made up the beadwork. They were blue, red, green, and white and were sewn together in a circle with a turtle in the middle.

"I have a turtle on mine too," Autumn said, glancing at her father.

"I don't remember doing turtle beadwork on yours," he said, and she smiled.

"Those are almost too small," she replied. "Aunt Jessie helped me make new ones. I beaded turtles and sewed them on."

She went to get them, and Autumn's parents each took turns looking at the moccasins. In the meantime, Jessie started to put dinner on the table and then called everyone to take a seat.

Autumn didn't know what to expect now at dinnertime. Before, it was a time her parents always fought. She didn't want to go through that again.

She glanced at Jessie, took a deep breath, and sat down.

Time to Reconnect

To her surprise, dinner went well and there was plenty of conversation going on. Autumn was smiling, and Jessie noticed Tom was relaxed and seemed happy. Melissa even smiled here and there, and then laughed outright when Autumn told them about something funny that happened in school.

After dinner, Jessie and Autumn cleaned up, and Melissa and Tom went into the living room to talk. They raised their voices in anger a couple of times, which made Autumn nervous, but Jessie put a reassuring hand on her shoulder and she nodded. She knew her parents had jumped right from heated arguments to the divorce. There were bound to be things that had to be worked out.

Sam sat in the corner of the kitchen playing with his blocks and little toy cars. After a moment, Melissa came in and picked him up.

"Autumn, your father wants to talk to you," she said. Autumn walked into the living room and saw her father sitting in his usual chair. It made her smile.

"Sit down, honey. I want to talk with you about school."

"Okay."

"I hear they have discovered you're dyslexic and that you're on some kind of education plan."

"Yes."

"How are things going?"

"Fine."

"No problems then with your schoolwork?"

"No."

He nodded and then reached into his pocket to take out a phone.

"I talked to your mother, and she said it was all right to give you this."

He handed her the phone, and she reached out and took it.

"Mom said I was not getting a phone until my sixteenth birthday," said Autumn, frowning.

"I know, but we talked about it, and I pointed out that with my work hours, it would be easier if I could just call you when I had the chance." He looked down at the floor now.

"I have been a terrible father. I haven't called or tried to come and see you after your mother and I split up. I'm so sorry."

"So, you think buying me a phone will make up for that?"

"No . . . I know it won't. But I wanted you to know you could call me anytime. I programmed my number into your phone already. It's under 'Dad.' I'm paying for the bill too. I just wanted to be sure we don't ever lose contact again." He looked over at her and tried to smile. "I love you, Autumn. I'm so sorry about all this. I hope to do better in the future."

"Why didn't you ever call me or come and see Sam or me?" Autumn bit her lip. "Did we do something wrong? I know you were mad at Mom, but . . ."

"No, no. Nothing like that."

"Then why?"

He sighed, trying to find the right words.

"Your mother and I were in such a bad place, I just wanted to get away from it all and clear my head. After some time had gone by, I realized I had just dumped my kids, and I was afraid you wouldn't want to see me again." He looked down at the floor again. "I guess it was easier to just hide away and pretend everything was fine instead of facing the truth."

"The truth?"

"The truth is, I was just a high school dropout with no prospects, and your mother could do better."

"But she loves you."

"I know that now. I finally *listened* to what she was telling me. You see, I saw her smiling and talking to my friend Benny, and I thought there was something going on between them."

Autumn shifted uncomfortably in her seat. "Wait, Dad, you don't have to tell me all this."

"Yes, I do, because it's about time I come clean about some things. I already talked to your mother, and I think you're old enough to know what happened."

He glanced over at her and she nodded reluctantly.

"Well, to make a long story short, I thought your mother was cheating on me. One of my friends tried to make trouble for her and told me that she was, and when I saw her with Benny, well . . . Anyway, I jumped to what I now know was the wrong conclusion. I wouldn't listen to anything your mother said, and then I let my insecurities get the best of me. I ran out the door and never looked back. I let my lawyer talk to hers and tried to get on with my life."

"Mom would never . . ."

"I know that now. I found out my friend had lied to me because he wanted to be with her. He tried to get her to go out with him afterward, but she wasn't having any of that." He smiled faintly. "She didn't want to be with anyone but me."

He got up and started to pace. "I have made such a mess with my life and my lack of self-confidence." He glanced over at her now.

"I'm so glad you found yours. You tried out for that play? You'll get in; I'm sure of it. I'm so glad you took a different road than I did."

"What do you mean?"

"You had problems. But when you realized there was nowhere to hide from them, you came out fighting for the life you wanted. You didn't hide yourself away from the world. You went out and confronted it head on."

"Thanks to Aunt Jessie."

Her father stopped in front of her now. "Yeah, she's a special person. I don't know what I would do without her. My beautiful cloud. She knew if she didn't come and pick me up, I wouldn't have come here tonight. She told me it was time to stop being a coward and own up to my part in the mess my marriage was in."

"Yeah, she seems to be right all the time," grumbled Autumn, and her father nodded and then grinned at the expression on his daughter's face.

"And I call her my 'beautiful cloud' too," she added.

She slipped the phone into her pocket and reached out to hug her dad.

"Can you stay?" she asked, and he shook his head.

"No, but I will be back next weekend. I'm going to start seeing you guys every other weekend."

"Okay." Autumn pulled away and sighed.

"What is it?"

"I wish we could see you all the time."

"You know I work."

"Well, yes, but . . ."

"Listen," he said, pulling her close again, "I plan to work on your mother. I know she still loves me. Maybe I can fix this mess and come home permanently."

Autumn grinned and hugged him again. "I sure hope so."

"Me too."

Her father broke away and went to say goodbye to everyone. He pulled Melissa in for a quick kiss, which made her blush and made Jessie and Autumn grin. Then he reached down to give Sam a kiss on the forehead and winked at Autumn.

"Call me," he said, and she nodded with a smile.

And then, with one last smile for each of them, he left.

Surprise, Surprise

Autumn got the lead. *The lead!*

She was standing in the hallway, staring at the door the cast list was posted on. Her name was on it, and across from it was the name of the lead part.

She blinked several times, wondering if she was once again reading something wrong. But the voice of Sydney behind her was as clear as a bell.

"The lead? She got the *lead*?"

Sydney turned to her friends Bree and Jayden and shook her head.

"Can you believe that? How did she manage to get that?"

"She was the best person for it," said Miss Jenkins, coming up behind them. She smiled at Autumn. "Pick up your script today and start memorizing your lines. There's quite a few of them."

"All right," Autumn replied, eyeing Sydney.

"Should I come and pick up a script?" asked Sydney. "I have been cast too."

"You have been cast in the ensemble," said Miss Jergens. "You will have a couple of costume changes but no actual lines. You won't need a script."

"I have no lines?"

Her teacher shook her head. "And I don't need you to come to every rehearsal. I will get a schedule to everyone soon."

Sydney and her friends watched the teacher walk away and then turned back to find Autumn had left as well. They watched her walk into a class down the hall and then turned to glance at each other.

"That girl . . . she has a part and I don't?" hissed Sydney. "That's ridiculous. I'm going to talk to my father about this."

"He won't be able to help you."

Sydney turned to look at Bree.

"What are you talking about? Of course he will."

"Nope," said Jayden. "He is not involved with the theater department."

"That doesn't matter," scoffed Sydney. He is on the school board and . . ."

"It won't matter." Bree sighed and shifted her books to the other arm. "Look, why don't you just leave Autumn alone? How much trouble do you want to get into? You've already been yelled at once."

"Yeah, by her aunt who doesn't matter," replied Sydney. "I don't care what she says."

"Well, we aren't getting into trouble for you," stated Bree. She started to walk away. "I'm leaving her alone."

"Me too," said Jayden, and Sydney watched them both walk away.

"You guys are idiots," she yelled. "Who needs you anyway?"

"What are you yelling about?" asked Miss Jergens, coming out of her classroom. "Get to class. The bell has already rung."

"But—"

"No buts."

"I—"

"Go!" Miss Jergens pointed down the hall, and Sydney snapped her mouth closed and headed in that direction.

As Sydney entered the classroom and sat down, her teacher looked up.

"Where have you been?" he asked. "The bell rang five minutes ago."

"I was talking to Miss Jergens."

"I see. Well, sit down. I have a class to teach."

Sydney sat down and clenched her teeth. She didn't care what anyone said, Autumn was not going to play the lead in the play. She would see to that.

When Autumn got home from school, she found Aunt Jessie in her room sewing jingles on the dress. She plopped down next to her and grinned.

"I got in."

"You got in the play? Oh, I'm so excited for you!" Jessie reached out to hug her. "What part did you get?"

"The lead."

Jessie pulled away to look at her. "They gave you the lead? I am so proud of you. I can't wait for your mom and dad to hear."

"How's the dress coming along?" Autumn asked. "I'm going to need it in a few weeks."

"We're going to have to step up working on it," replied Jessie. "Let me see your script."

Autumn pulled out the script and they both read through it, identifying the parts Autumn may have a problem reading. Then Jessie gave it back to her and continued sewing.

"Tell you what. You start memorizing your lines and I will keep sewing. We'll get the dress done in time for the play; don't worry about that."

"Are you sure? I would like to help do the sewing."

"I will start again after dinner," replied Jessie. "If your homework is done, you can help me then."

"All right."

A few days later, rehearsals began for the play. Autumn already had some of her lines memorized, and Miss Jergens was pleased.

Sydney was not pleased. When she told her father about the play and that *she* should have gotten the lead, not Autumn, he just shrugged and told her to deal with the situation herself.

Now she was standing backstage watching the girl she hated get stage direction for the part she wanted. It was unbelievable.

Autumn knew Sydney was mad. Every time she glanced over in that direction, Sydney glared at her. Even Miss Jergens noticed and addressed Sydney more than once about the situation.

"Sydney, you are in danger of getting booted out of this play if you don't stop this behavior," said Miss Jergens. "We are a cast and support each other. Take your attitude elsewhere."

All that conversation did was make Sydney more mad and Autumn uneasy. From that day on, Autumn worked very hard to be sure she was never alone with Sydney. She never stood by her if she could help it, and never spoke to her.

The teacher noticed, and two weeks before they were about to perform the play, Sydney's parents were called. They showed up at the theater during rehearsal and stood backstage with Sydney and Miss Jergens while the issue was discussed.

"I would like to speak to Autumn if I could," said Sydney's father, eyeing Sydney.

Autumn was called backstage, and she went reluctantly. The others sitting in the theater-style seats knew what was going on. She was so embarrassed.

"Autumn," said Miss Jergens, "this is Mr. Coffman. He would like to speak to you about what has been going on between you and Sydney."

Autumn swallowed hard and nodded, glancing up at Mr. Coffman.

"Has my daughter been harassing you?" he asked, staring at her with no expression on his face. Autumn looked away and nodded.

"And what have you been doing to upset her?"

"Mr. Coffman," interrupted Miss Jergens, "I already told you—"

"Nothing."

Mr. Coffman's eyes narrowed. "Nothing? You mean to tell me that you haven't been doing a thing to upset my daughter? I find that hard to believe. My daughter is a good, kind person, but she stands up for herself. I taught her that. She's not going to let anyone tease her or—"

"She is."

Miss Jergens frowned, and Mr. Coffman paused a moment.

"She is what?" asked her teacher, and Autumn smiled at Sydney.

"I know she is a good, kind person. My aunt Jessie says everyone is deep down. But she has been pushing me in the halls, teasing me about my speech problems, and"—she glanced over at Sydney—"hates that I was cast in the lead and she was not." She took a deep breath and then added, "My aunt says behavior like this starts at home."

"Autumn!" said her teacher. "That wasn't very nice to say."

"Apparently the child was not taught any manners," replied Mr. Coffman angrily. "A child should not speak to an adult like that."

"She's right."

"What?" Mr. Coffman turned to look at his wife. "What did you say?"

She shook her head. "This is a conversation we should have privately."

"We're going to have it right here and now!" he replied. "I don't care who . . ."

Miss Jergens took Autumn and stepped away. They could still hear Sydney's parents, who were arguing loudly.

"She learned it from you, Roger. And furthermore . . ."

Miss Jergens didn't think anyone else should be hearing that conversation, and so she pulled

Sydney down the stage stairs to give the cast notes regarding the play. A few moments later, Sydney and her parents came onstage and gestured over to Miss Jergens and Autumn. They both reluctantly walked to the stage and looked up at them.

"I'm sorry," said Sydney, not looking at her. "It won't happen again."

Miss Jergens glanced over at Autumn, who nodded.

"And I'm also sorry," said Mr. Coffman. He held himself proudly, and by the look on his face, he didn't seem to be sorry, but Autumn nodded again anyway.

Sydney went to sit down with the cast and didn't speak again for the rest of rehearsal. Autumn felt sorry for her. Her parents had obviously embarrassed her by their outburst.

A moment later Autumn was called onstage, and Sydney followed quietly behind. Autumn glanced into Sydney's face, but Sydney looked away, still angry.

Autumn sighed. It was going to be a long rehearsal.

CHAPTER 12

The Big Night

Tom was looking through the program in his hands.

"*The Jingle Dress,*" he read out loud, "by Samantha Jergens." He opened it and grinned when he saw who was playing the lead.

He had arrived early and found a seat toward the back. He still wasn't sure how he would be received by Autumn and didn't want to sit too close where she could see him. If she was upset he was there, it could mess up her performance.

He had seen her several times over the last few weeks, and things were going all right. He was careful not to rush things, and Autumn must have felt the same because she hadn't hugged him since the time he had come for dinner.

"What are you doing way back here?"

Tom looked up to see his sister staring down at him, shaking her head.

"The family's up front," she said, smiling. "Come on."

"Oh, I don't know . . ." The word "family" had made him nervous. He didn't think he could be considered as family anymore.

"Come on." Jessie pulled him up out of his seat and pushed him down the aisle. "We saved a seat for you."

"You did?"

"Of course."

"Why?"

Jessie stopped, and he noticed and turned to look at her.

"You aren't the sharpest tool in the shed," she said, shaking her head. "We all love you and want you with us."

"But, Melissa . . ."

"She is healing, Tom. They all are. You can help by making sure they know how much you want to be considered a part of this family."

He nodded. "I do." He cleared his throat as they started down the aisle again. "Thanks, Jessie."

She smiled as she showed him to his seat. Melissa glanced at him and nodded, and a moment later the play began. One of Autumn's classmates came out onstage and sat down. He carried a flute, raised it, and started to play.

The first half of the play introduced the girl and her family, and it ended when she became ill.

It lasted about a half hour, and by intermission, Sam was starting to fuss. Melissa reached over to take him from Jessie, but Tom grabbed him and pulled him close.

"I got this," he said with a smile, but Melissa looked doubtful.

He shook his head. "Have some faith. I *am* his father, you know."

Melissa opened her mouth to say something but caught Jessie's shake of her head and closed it again. She nodded and gave him a smile.

The play seemed to be going well, thought Miss Jergens, glancing at the audience. She gave everyone a smile as she talked to families milling about while her crew moved furniture around on the stage. She caught Autumn's mother's gaze and nodded, and Melissa smiled back at her.

Autumn stood in the dressing room staring at herself in the mirror. She hardly recognized the girl staring back at her.

Her hair was pulled back into two braids that were tied off with red leather straps. Her Jingle Dress had been completed a couple of days before the play opened, and it was beautiful. Three hundred and sixty-five jingles were sewn side by side and hit against each other when she walked.

"You can't sneak up on anybody, can you?"

Autumn saw Sydney enter behind her, and the two girls stared at each other in the mirror. Sydney was dressed in a simple leather dress with fringe. Her hair was also braided.

"No, I guess not," answered Autumn, glancing around to see if anyone else was listening. She still didn't like to be alone with Sydney.

"Your aunt Jessie did a great job on the beadwork," commented Sydney, and Autumn's eyes raised up in surprise.

"Thank you. I . . . I will tell her," she replied. "But I helped."

"You helped? What does that mean?"

"Jessie made the dress. We both sewed on the jingles and did the beadwork."

"Really."

Autumn nodded.

"That's hard to believe."

"Why?"

Sydney shrugged. "You took woodshop. I didn't know you sewed."

"Aunt Jessie taught me. My father also does beadwork."

"I saw him in the audience. Your folks back together now?"

"They're working on it."

Sydney nodded and walked away.

"Five minutes," said Kelsey the stage manager. "Take your places."

Autumn took a deep breath and turned around, following the others out of the dressing room.

On the way to where she entered the stage, she went over and over the Jingle Dress dance steps in her mind. Jessie had taught her the traditional way to do them, and they had spent hours practicing them in her bedroom.

Autumn took a deep breath and entered, saying her lines. Then she started to dance.

The sequins on her dress glittered as she moved, and the jingles sounded like Santa's sleigh as she bounced and danced across the floor. When she was finished, there was thunderous applause and she smiled, in spite of trying to stay in character.

When the play ended, Autumn took her place in the curtain call. She was really happy with her performance. She had hesitated in a few places but managed to get the words out without calling too much attention to the fact that she couldn't say her s's correctly. She had not missed any lines.

When the curtain call began, Sydney started to walk out but tripped on her way to take her bow. Autumn reached out and caught her without attracting too much attention. Sydney glanced at her in surprise, nodded, and then took her bow.

Sydney's parents were in the front row. Her mother was clapping and smiling while her father was just clapping. Autumn wondered if the man ever smiled, and wondered for the first time what it was like to live with parents like that. She glanced over at Sydney, who went back to her place in line. She looked unhappy, and Autumn felt bad for her.

Maybe that's why Sydney was so mean, she thought, as the cast clasped hands and took their final bow. Maybe she was upset with her father and took it out on other people.

She looked over, caught Sydney's gaze, and gave her a smile. Sydney frowned as the curtain dropped.

Life Can't Always Be Perfect

After the play was over, Autumn's family went out for ice cream. They piled into the SUV, and Autumn smiled at the coziness of it all.

Several minutes later they arrived at Autumn's favorite ice-cream parlor. She ordered and then sat down with her family to wait.

It took awhile to get everyone's treats made up, but eventually Autumn was shoving spoonfuls of mint ice cream into her mouth as she glanced around the table.

Her father sat next to her mother with his arm around her. She was smiling up at him, and he hesitated a moment before bending down to kiss her on the forehead. She blushed and then looked away.

Jessie was wiping the ice cream dripping off Sam's chin. She caught Autumn's gaze and smiled.

"You did a wonderful job, honey," she said, helping Sam with his spoon. "I was so proud of you."

"Everyone loved the dress," Autumn replied. "It was so beautiful."

"That's because you were wearing it," answered Jessie, and Autumn smiled.

"No more problems with Sydney?"

Autumn shook her head.

"Hmm . . . I hope that is the end of it then," said Jessie.

"Me too." She paused and then added, "You know, she talked to me today."

Jessie's eyes narrowed. "About what?"

"No . . . no, she was really nice. I mean . . . well . . . as nice as she can be, I guess."

Jessie grinned. "What did she say?"

"She liked the dress."

"Really? She paid you a compliment?"

Autumn nodded and then took another spoonful of ice cream.

"You know, I feel bad for her."

"What? Why is that?"

"I saw her parents in the audience. Her mother was smiling and clapping, but her father was only clapping. He doesn't seem like a very nice person."

"Just because he wasn't smiling?"

"No. He talked to me a few weeks ago about what was going on with Sydney. He thought I was harassing her."

"Well, I hope you told him different," replied Jessie with a frown. "You know, I saw what she was doing to you in the hall. Maybe I could go talk to him and . . ."

Autumn shook her head. "He wouldn't listen. Like I said, he doesn't seem very nice."

Jessie sighed. "Well, I'm sorry to hear that. I feel bad for Sydney now, although that doesn't excuse her behavior."

There was a pause, and then Autumn sighed, setting down her spoon.

"I hear you are leaving to go back to your apartment."

Jessie nodded. "They are finished with the renovations."

"When are you going back?" asked Tom.

"Monday."

"That's only two days from now," said Melissa. "You have to go so soon?"

Jessie smiled at her and then glanced at her brother.

"Oh, I think you're going to be able to handle things from here on out," she replied.

"I don't know . . ." Melissa bit her lip and Tom raised her face to his.

"We'll be fine, Melissa."

"I . . . I don't know . . ."

"I do."

Autumn watched them for a moment, and then turned back to Jessie.

"I wish you didn't have to go."

Jessie smiled. "Even clouds float away. You have a phone now. Call me whenever you want. Maybe you can make a trip to the city to see me this summer."

"Could I? I would love that!"

"Me too." She glanced over at Tom and Melissa. "Give them some time, honey. Hopefully things will turn out the way you want them to. But if they don't, just be grateful for what you have. They both love you very much."

"I know, but . . ."

Jessie smiled and took her hand.

"An Ojibwa elder once told me, 'One thing we know for sure is that we all have a limited number of days here on earth.'"

"I know that, but . . ."

"So each day we can either find something to complain about or something to be grateful for. It's really up to us."

Autumn dropped Jessie's hand and sat back in her chair. She thought about everything she had gone through with Sydney's bullying and her speech issues. Her thoughts went back to how she didn't want Jessie to come and now she didn't want her to leave. She even had the lead in the school play! In a very short time, she had come a long way.

Autumn looked around the table at her family. Things weren't ever going to be perfect, she thought, but maybe they weren't meant to be. She would always have her speech issues, and not everyone was going to like her.

She smiled and reached over to give Aunt Jessie's hand a squeeze.

Nope, things were never going to be perfect. But she was okay with that.

RESOURCES

NEUHAUS ACADEMY

neuhausacademy.org

Neuhaus Academy helps teenage and adult learners improve their reading, spelling, and comprehension skills through simple online instruction. All lessons are individually tailored to each person's specific needs so that learners can work at their own pace. The courses are always free for learners and can be customized by instructors to promote and ensure a successful outcome.

FRIENDS OF QUINN

friendsofquinn.com/for-young-adults

Friends of Quinn is an online community that connects and inspires people affected by learning differences. It offers resources, social networking, and support for young adults with learning differences and for the people who love them. The website was founded by Quinn Bradlee, filmmaker and author of *A Different Life*, a book about growing up with learning differences.

SMART KIDS WITH LEARNING DISABILITIES
smartkidswithld.org

Smart Kids with Learning Disabilities aims to educate, guide, and inspire parents of children with learning disabilities or ADHD. Its goal is to help parents realize their children's significant gifts and talents and to show that with love, guidance, and the right support, their children can live happy and productive lives.

UNDERSTOOD
for learning & attention issues
understood.org

The mission of Understood is to support the millions of parents whose children are struggling with learning and attention issues. The organization strives to empower parents and help them better understand their children's issues and experiences. With this knowledge, parents can then make effective choices that propel their children from simply coping to truly thriving.

CHILD MIND INSTITUTE
childmind.org

The Child Mind Institute is an independent, national nonprofit dedicated to transforming the lives of children and families struggling with mental health and learning disorders. Its objectives are to deliver the highest standards of care, advance the science of the developing brain, and empower parents, professionals, and policymakers to support children whenever and wherever they need it most.

ABOUT THE AUTHOR

KIM SIGAFUS is an award-winning Ojibwa writer and Illinois Humanities Road Scholar speaker. She has coauthored two 7th Generation books in the Native Trailblazers series of biographies, including *Native Elders: Sharing Their Wisdom* and the award-winning *Native Writers: Voices of Power.* Her fiction work includes The Mida, an eight-volume series about a mystically powerful time-traveling carnival owned by an Ojibwa woman. Kim's family is from the White Earth Indian Reservation in northern Minnesota. She resides with her husband in Freeport, Illinois. For more information, visit kimberlysigafus.com.